I Saw It in the Garden

By Martin Brennan
Illustrated by Michael Glenn Monroe

Happy gardening!

mitten press

Michael Monroe

All inquiries should be addressed to:
Mitten Press
An imprint of Ann Arbor Media Group LLC
2500 S. State Street
Ann Arbor, MI 48104

Printed and bound in Canada.

10   9   8   7   6   5   4   3   2   1

Library of Congress Cataloging-in-Publication Data

Brennan, Martin, 1966-
I saw it in the garden / by Martin Brennan ; illustrated by Michael Glenn Monroe.
     p. cm.
Summary: From the joy of early spring to the return of Jack Frost, a young girl and her grandfather tend a garden filled with plants and the host of creatures that make a home there.
ISBN-13: 978-1-58726-296-8 (hardcover : alk. paper)
ISBN-10: 1-58726-296-7 (hardcover : alk. paper)
[1. Gardening--Fiction. 2. Grandfathers--Fiction. 3. Seasons--Fiction.
4. Stories in rhyme.] I. Monroe, Michael Glenn, ill. II. Title.
PZ8.3.B74552Ias 2006
[E]--dc22
                              2005034184

APRIL 1st

My grandpa told me once
all he'd come to know
of what a person needs to do
to help a garden grow.

"Find a sturdy shovel,
proper boots, and gloves.
Hope for rain—but not too much
and plant your seeds with love."

"Then keep your eyes wide open.
You might just be in awe."
I did just what my grandpa said
and this is what I saw...

APRIL 11*th*

Springtime is zing-time,
spin-your-partner-swing-time.
Wake the snoozin'
black-eyed Susan.
Winter's over sing-time.

APRIL 18*th*

An itsy bitsy spec of life
sleeps inside the ground,
in the dark all by itself
without a sight or sound.

It's never seen the sun before,
and tell me if you know—
who tells the sleepy little seeds,
wake up, it's time to grow?

MAY 6*th*

*T*he sun is the greatest magician
the world has ever found.
He doesn't pull rabbits from top hats;
he pulls life up from the ground.

MAY 15*th*

*M*y watering can is filled with rain
all the way up to the spout.
And when I tip it just a bit,
the rain falls gently out.

MAY 26*th*

I ran to my grandpa as fast as I could,
jumped up and down and shouted,
"It's here grandpa. Quick, come see.
One of the plants has sprouted!"

Together we hurried out to the garden
and dropping to our knees,
we eyed the miracle there in the ground—
such joy from two tiny leaves!

JUNE 12*th*

*D*andelions stalk me daily;
they cause me so much trouble.
I beat them back the best I can,
but they just come back double.

*O*h no,
the weeds grow.
And though I hoe,
they grow and grow.

I hoe.
     They grow.
I hoe.
     They grow.
Hoe.
     Grow.
Hoe.
     Grow.

     Grow.

GROW.

GROW!

JUNE 23*rd*

A slippety, sloggety bug
ate my tomato plants down to the nub.
He ate and ate and grew so fat.
Grandpa caught that bug
and now

he's . . .

SPLAT!

JULY *4th*

*T*o be a bee seems to be
a job for me because
I'd get to dance in flowers
and laugh and sing and buzz.

JULY 19*th*

Once there lived an apple core
of use to no one anymore,
and so I chucked him out the door.
From there his story grows.

He landed on a compost heap
and quietly began to weep,
until he cried himself to sleep
and slowly decomposed.

Though it looks as though he's dead,
he's quite alive, and so it's said,
he's moved into a flower bed
and lives inside a rose.

JULY 29th

Aphids were in the garden,
    eating whatever they pleased.
And though I asked them nicely,
    they kept on munching leaves.

I called my friends the ladybugs
to come and share some tea.
I served them scones and marmalade
and aphid fricassee.

AUGUST 2nd

*T*he scarecrow hangs upon a post
keeping birds away.
Would I keep smiling if I hung
upon a post all day?

AUGUST 10*th*

*H*ow does a pole bean grow so high
   without any fingers, toes, or eyes?

Would it climb to the sky if it could?
   Does it ever get tired? I think I would.

AUGUST 18*th*

*I*f you swallow melon seeds,
so the legend goes,
the seeds will settle in your craw,
and there the seeds will grow.

I told this to my cousin Al,
who came to stay the night.
But he just laughed at me and said,
"Ah, it'll be all right."

Al ate one,
Al ate ten,
Al ate twenty,
thirty…
then,
from his nose a leaf crept out.
Cousin Al began to sprout!

AUGUST 30*th*

*G*randpa was tired. I was, too.
And though there was plenty we still had to do—
　　　like corn to pick and beans to can,
　　and finish painting our vegetable stand.
We found ourselves a patch of shade
　　　　and drank two quarts of lemonade.

　　　　　Grandpa closed his eyes and said,
　　　　　　"I remember, once, a poem I read,
　　　　　Now I lay me down to sleep
　　　　　　I pray the Lord my soul to keep…"
　　　　But Gramps could not say anymore.
　　　　　　How could he? He'd begun to snore.

OCTOBER 12*th*

*L*eaves are falling from the trees.
Winter starts to whisper.
Jack Frost dances in the grass,
and every night feels crisper.

Days grow short. The sun cools off.
The geese fly high above.
The time has come to put away
the shovel, boots, and gloves.

Grandpa sighed and I did, too
when we closed the gate.
The garden that we'll grow next year,
well … I can hardly wait.

Seeds really want to grow!
They're just waiting for you
 to help them get water, light, food, and air.

Step 1 Prepare your soil. Remove any grass or plants growing in your garden and loosen the soil as deep as possible with a small shovel or digging fork. This allows air into the soil and makes it easy for your plant's roots to grow.

Step 2 Add some compost. Adding compost to the top 4 inches of soil will provide food for your plants in the soil. Break up clumps and rake the surface smooth.

Step 3 Plant your seeds. Big seeds need to be planted as deep as your finger is long in the ground. Small seeds are planted shallowly, just as deep as your fingernail. Check the back of your seed pack for more information.

Step 4 Water your seeds gently. Keep the soil moist all the time until the seedlings sprout. After that, you can let the soil surface dry out between waterings. Be sure not to drown the seeds or plants with too much water.

Step 5 Visit your plants every day to check on their progress. Stick your finger into the soil to see if it is moist. Remove any weeds that might sprout up to compete with your plants for water, light, food, and air.

Keep your eyes wide open!
You might just be amazed by what you see in your garden.